December 2018

This book belongs to:

Whitaker and Aspen

May all your Christmases be magical!

Love,
Grandma & Gramps

For Mum and Dad
Visit the author's website! ericjames.co.uk

Written by Eric James
Illustrated by Simon Mendez
Cover design by Sourcebooks, Inc.
Art direction by John Aardema
Internal design and hand lettering by Travis Hasenour
Internal images © Freepik, David M. Schrader/Shutterstock

Copyright © Hometown World Ltd. 2017

Published by Sourcebooks Jabberwocky, an imprint of Sourcebooks, Inc.
P.O. Box 4410, Naperville, Illinois 60567-4410
(630) 961-3900
Fax: (630) 961-2168
sourcebooks.com

Source of Production: China (LPG)
Date of Production: July 2017
Run Number: HTW_PO240417
10 9 8 7 6 5 4 3 2 1

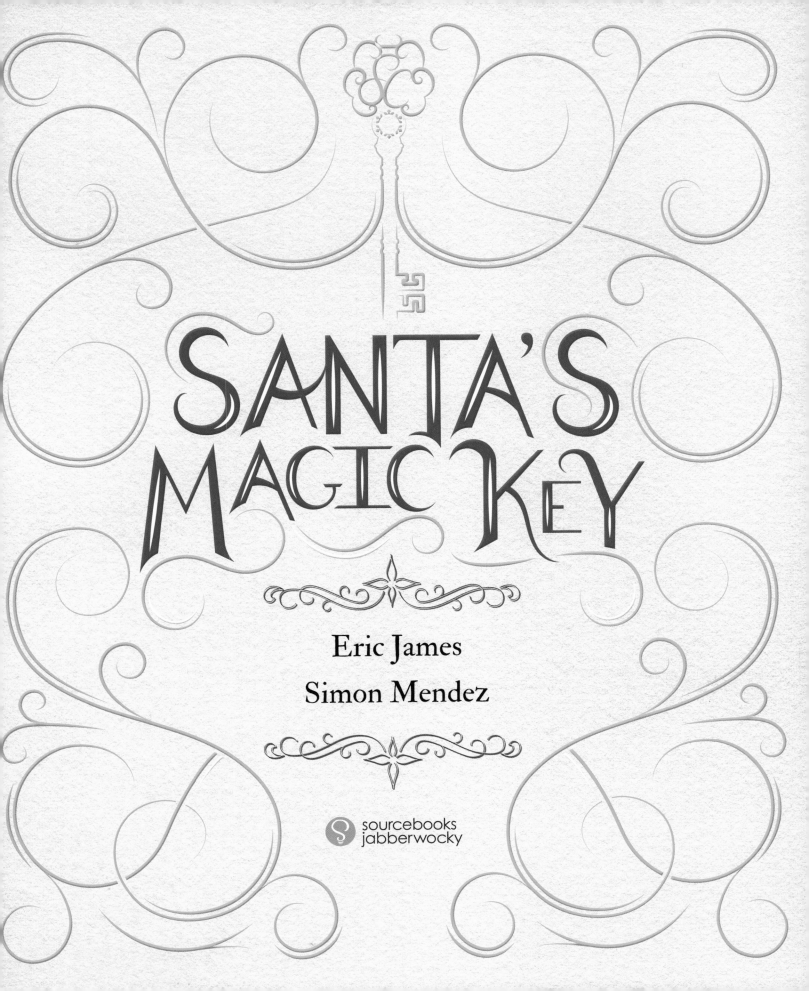

SANTA'S MAGIC KEY

Eric James

Simon Mendez

sourcebooks
jabberwocky

I didn't notice it was missing until Christmas Eve...and only then because I was looking for a place to hang my stocking in our new home.

Everybody knows that when Santa delivers presents, he comes down the chimney. But my new home didn't *have* a chimney, so how would Santa get in?

I had to write him a letter, and quickly! It wouldn't be long before Santa was loading up his sleigh and setting off!

My heart was pounding as
I rushed out the door and
headed to the post office.

Maybe they had a last-
minute delivery of mail that
could reach Santa in time.

"Please be open. *Please!*
I've been good all year!"

But when I got there,
the lights were out and
nobody was inside.

I was too late!

How would I get my letter
to Santa now?

Sorry WE'RE CLOSED

Santa Claus
North Pole
HoHo HoHo

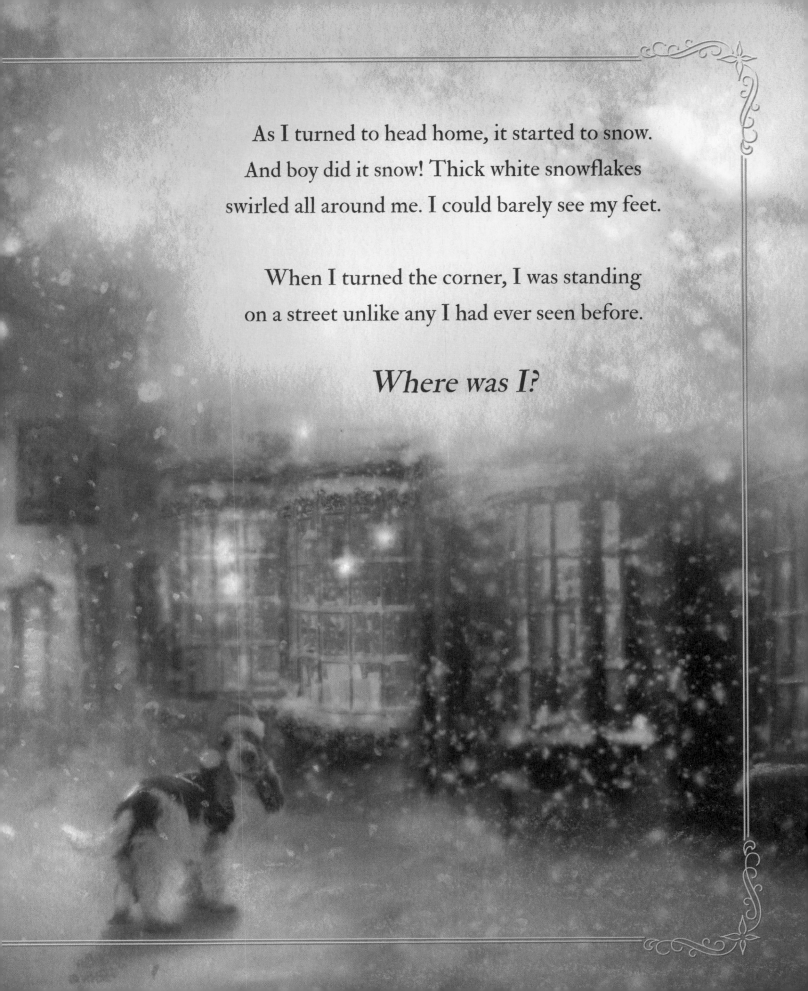

As I turned to head home, it started to snow.
And boy did it snow! Thick white snowflakes
swirled all around me. I could barely see my feet.

When I turned the corner, I was standing
on a street unlike any I had ever seen before.

Where was I?

Christmas carols drifted on the air and a horse-drawn sleigh whooshed by.

A brightly lit window drew me toward a shop halfway down the street.

I cupped my hands against the
frosty glass and peered in.

Toys lined each wall.
The biggest Christmas tree I had ever
seen stood in one corner, with dozens
of neatly wrapped packages beneath it.

But the most wonderful thing of
all was the sign in the window.

As I pushed open the door, a little bell tinkled above my head.

"Can I help you?" asked a cheery man with a white beard.

"Yes, please," I said. "I have to get this to Santa as soon as possible. He needs to know that I haven't got a chimney!"

I handed him the letter. "Will Santa get it in time?" I asked.

The shopkeeeper's big eyes
twinkled. "Oh, yes," he said.
"I *guarantee* it."

I thanked him, but as I turned to leave he called after me.

"Just a moment! I can't let you go out into the snow without
a coat." He handed me a large coat with white trim.
"No need to return it," he said, "I have a new one now."

"Merry Christmas!" he said, opening the door for me.

"Merry Christmas to you too, sir," I replied.

I walked out into the freezing snow. I had just reached the street corner when my fingers touched something slim and metal in the coat pocket.

It was a *key*.

"This must belong to the shopkeeper," I thought. I turned around to return it, but the street I had just come from was *no longer there!*

As soon as I got home, I hung up my
stocking at the bottom of the stairs,
and put a big cookie and a glass of milk on the
table, hoping that Santa would be able to get in.

Finally I jumped into bed. But I couldn't sleep!
What if Santa didn't get my letter? What if the
shopkeeper needed his key? I had an idea—I sat
up in bed and wrote a note.

I padded downstairs and hung the key on
the front door, with my note to the shopkeeper.
With any luck, he would pass by and see it.

I had done as much as I could. I went back to
bed and soon fell into a deep sleep.

On Christmas morning, I woke very early and ran downstairs.

On the table there were lots of cookie crumbs and an empty glass. Santa had gotten inside...but how?

Just then I spotted my stocking, bulging with gifts and something shiny poking out from the top.

It was the *key!*

I pulled out the key and
with it came a note.

December 25th

Thank you for hanging my key on the door.

Keep believing in the magic of Christmas, and don't forget to put it out every year!

Santa
XOXO

Suddenly I noticed something I hadn't seen before.
The key had the initials S.C.

Didn't the key belong to the *shopkeeper*?
I ran to the closet and pulled out the shopkeeper's coat.
Inside, I spotted a name tag.

I kept that coat, and we lived in that house for many years. Each Christmas Eve, I hung the key on the front door, and every Christmas morning I woke to find that Santa had visited! Even when we moved into a house with a chimney, I still hung the key outside and Santa put it back in my stocking before he left.

I'm grown up now so Santa no longer needs to visit me. I've kept the key as a reminder of my wonderful adventure, but now I think it's time to pass it on to someone special.

It's for *you!*

Hang it on your front door each year, and as
long as you keep believing in the magic of
Christmas, the key will let Santa in.